To My Glover

Wishing You Hope & Joy

Elizabeth

Praise for *The Blue Elephant*

"*The Blue Elephant* is a wondrous children's book full of insight, discovery, and compassion. It deals with a young person's grief in a way that explains the confusion, sadness, and self-doubt that occurs in all of us. Joy's journey of self-discovery realistically deals with a child's dread of being different and the insecurity of her place in the world. It's heartfelt with a touch of magical interpretation."

—PATTI O. WHITE, Emmy Award-Winning Producer/Writer,
Former CBS News (*60 Minutes*, *CBS Reports*, *30 Minutes*),
Principal/Owner of FILMSTERS Television and Film production company,
Annapolis Film Festival Co-Founder and Festival Director

"*The Blue Elephant* is a beautiful story that helps children to make sense of their emotions after experiencing the death of someone they loved. The story demonstrates how sadness and joy can coexist in one's feelings and that the essence of life is found in hope. This powerful, yet simple story of Joy's journey through sadness helps children to understand that grief is a normal process and, by allowing themselves to experience their emotions, leads to greater understanding of their unique purpose in life."

—MICHAEL MCHALE, MHA, LNHA, President & CEO

"*The Blue Elephant* is a delightful story of how our sense of being different can lead us on a journey of self-discovery, friendship, loss, and giving back. Regardless of our age, Joy and Hope are companions who can support us on our journey through life."

—BEN MARCANTONIO, President & CEO, Hospice of the Chesapeake

"*The Blue Elephant* is a beautiful story of discovery and purpose in the midst of a confusing world. A story that encourages readers of all ages to remember that while there is sadness in every life, there is also hope and from hope joy can spring."

—JOSH BURNETT, Lead Pastor of Revolution Church, Annapolis, MD

"*The Blue Elephant* is a whimsical book and is beautifully illustrated in watercolor. It's a story of how young friends can help each other in times of grief, and find a sense of purpose in doing so. It's a sweet and gentle book on learning life lessons."

—DAVID HARTCORN, Author of *49 at 49: Portraiture in Two Mediums*

"This sweet and heartfelt story demonstrates the power of friendship, and how learning to cherish our uniqueness can result in our making a deep and lasting difference in the world."

—SARAH MONTGOMERY, Coordinator of Children and Family Programs at Chesapeake Life Center

"A lot of research supports the idea that our basic frameworks for life are set by age ten. Children's books matter. Good children's book matter more. Elizabeth Liechty has written a good one. I grew up in an age when "different" often carried any negative connotations. Different skin color. Different race. *The Blue Elephant* is an endearing and sweet tale that might modify some of our kid's basic frameworks for life. I like it because Elizabeth is not a professional writer. She's an amateur, a word we get from the Latin *amator* and the Italian *amatore*—lover. Elizabeth wrote *The Blue Elephant* out of love for kids. But don't feel bad if you like it as well. I did—and I'm well past the age of ten!"

—MIKE METZGER, CEO of the Clapham Institute

"A blue elephant named Joy and a butterfly named Hope—what else could any child want? But there's more—the insight that no matter what color you are, you have a unique purpose, something no one else can do. This book will charm you, make you wiser, and, yes, give you hope and joy."

—BARBARA BRADLEY HAGERTY, Author of *Life Reimagined*

A Story of Grief, Loss, and Friendship

The Blue Elephant

Written by **Elizabeth Ann Liechty** | Illustrated by **John "Charlie" Hanson**

A POST HILL PRESS BOOK

ISBN: 9781682617168

Illustrations by John "Charlie" Hanson
Interior design and composition by Greg Johnson/Textbook Perfect
Cover design and layout by Tricia Principe, principedesign.com

Post Hill Press
New York • Nashville
posthillpress.com

Printed in China

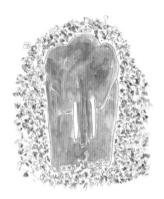

To my family and friends who have brought great joy and hope into my life. You know who you are, but a special thank you to:

Amy, my Joy. Karen, my beloved friend who shared my dream for *The Blue Elephant* since its inception when we first went to South Africa in 2007. Hillary, my Grace and inspirational creative friend. Lee, for believing in me and this story and bringing *The Blue Elephant* to life through the animated film. Sister Lynette and Joan with Brits Hospice and all the beautiful South African people and children as well as all the children and individuals at Hospice of the Chesapeake who inspired me to write this children's book.

Thank you all for being a part of my life's journey. My world would not be the same without all of you in it.

Hi. I'm Joy.

I've always been a little different.
I was born light blue instead of gray.
But the herd was so happy to have a little one,
they ignored my blue skin and named me *Joy*.

I tried my best to fit in.

One day grandmother, whom I loved
very much, died. As grief washed over me,
I saw that I was turning a deeper shade of blue.

That was awkward.

I snuck off to our watering hole,
hoping to scrub the color away.
No luck.

I tried rolling in the mud. It caked on my body and really helped a lot.

But the mud treatment was tiring—
sneaking to the watering hole every day.
I wasn't sure I could do this forever.

Then one day, things changed.
I was alone, rolling in the mud,
when a butterfly fluttered toward me.

"I'm Hope," she said, resting on my head.

She looked a bit . . . like a barrette.

Hope asked what I was doing.

I tried to explain, but Hope interrupted.
"Your blueness is much more beautiful than mud!
Without bright colors, I'd have no purpose in life!"

Hope told me about how butterflies love colorful flowers, flitting from bloom to bloom and moving pollen between plants, helping them make seeds so more flowers can grow. Hope was very proud of her purpose—helping create new life in the world.

Hope was quiet for a while.

"Do you know *your* life's purpose?" she said.

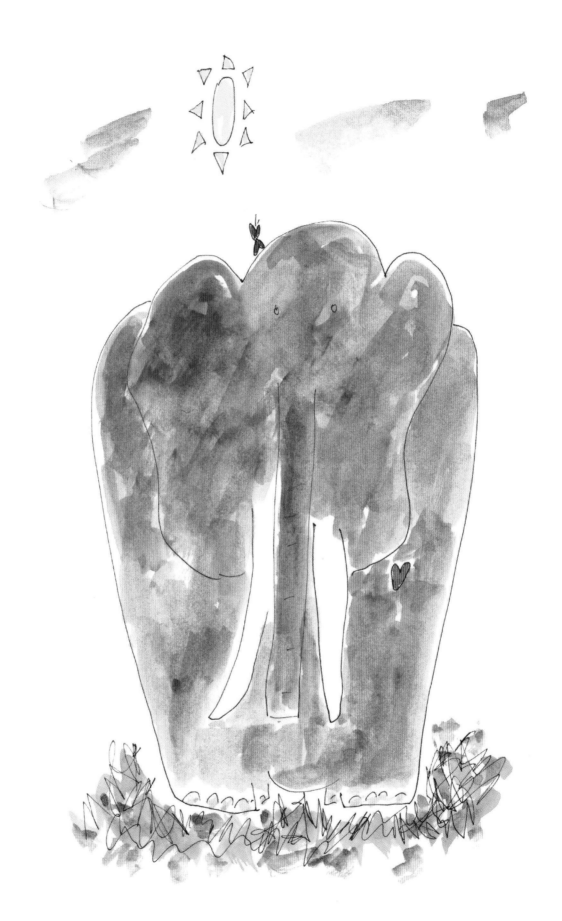

No one had ever asked me this before.

"What's a blue elephant's purpose?" I wondered.

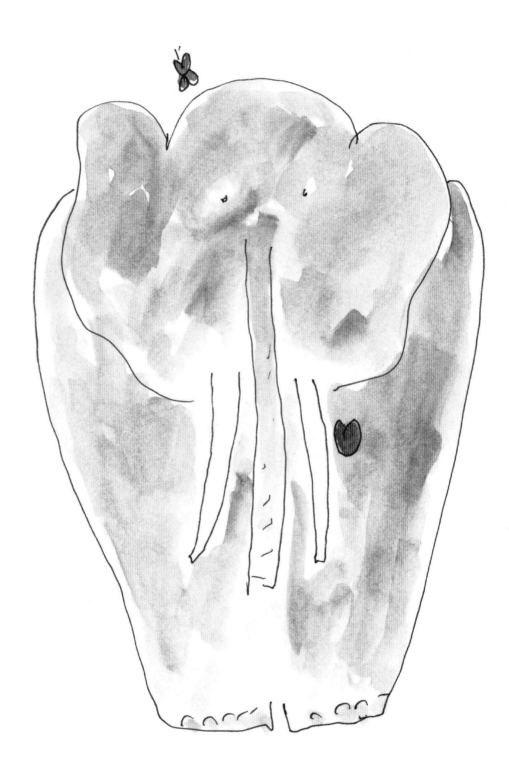

Hope found me the next day on my way to the watering hole. And she found me every day after that.

　　She would follow along, flitting and floating happily by my ear, trying to distract me from my mission.

Most days my new friend would flutter gracefully by my side until her chatter about my beautiful blue body made her tired. Then she would hitch a ride on my head. There she would stay quietly, for the longest time—my butterfly barrette.

One day, as we sat talking in the grass, I told Hope the story of Grandmother dying. I told her about my sadness, and about turning deeper blue. "Why didn't you tell me sooner?" she squeaked. "You express your grief through your blue hide! This will lead us to your purpose in life!"

"But my name is Joy," I reminded her. "What if I'm supposed to make everyone happy?" Hope paused. "As much as we wish those we love to feel good all the time, each of us grieves and carries sadness with us. It's part of life for all species, but most of us hide it on the inside, unlike you. The answer to your purpose will come," Hope reassured me. "Let's be quiet and see what happens. Sometimes stillness helps light the way."

I closed my eyes. For a while the only sound was the swish of my ears, swatting flies.

Then I heard something. It sounded like dripping, very far away.

"Do you hear that?" I whispered.

"What?" said Hope.

"...dripping..."

"No," said Hope, "but your ears are a bit bigger than mine. Listen closer."

I squeezed my eyes tight. Drip, drip, drip. I followed the sound in my mind. Somewhere, I realized, a child was grieving. The sadness was too great for the child's soul to bear. I could hear tears, I could hear a heart breaking. I let my imagination follow the sound—all the way to the child's side.

From that day forward, I met many children who were carrying too much grief. With Hope's help and a bit of practice, we found a way to visit these children in their dreams.

In dreamtime, I could be small and light and very, very gentle. Hope would stir a breeze with her wings, and I would float upon it to a child. I would lay my light like a feather on the child's heart, drawing out the sadness that was too heavy to bear. Night after night, I found grieving children.

Before long, though, I began to feel heavy. I was becoming a much deeper shade of blue. Hope worried that the weight of the children's grief was even more than an elephant could carry. She was right: I was getting too blue.

Hope did her best to help. "Take courage, dear heart," she would whisper.

When her words were not enough, she even helped me carry the sorrow. She tied a string to my trunk, and flapping her wings mightily, fluttered up, as though to lift me. Although I doubted she had the power at first—my dear friend had the strength to help me find my feet.

Over time, I learned that crying helped me feel better. When the blue was too much, I cried—tears so big and blue, they made lovely puddles that helped wildflowers to grow. Seeing how much Hope loved these blossoms brought me back to my name. Joy.

With my butterfly barrette, I had found my unique purpose in life. My best friend Hope had helped me learn that sadness is a part of everyone's life journey, but that we don't have to travel it alone. I am learning to trust this path of helping grieving children, even though I don't know where it will take me.

Meanwhile, we make quite a pair, Hope and I.
A dainty butterfly and a bright blue elephant,
as we stroll the beautiful meadows we've
created together.

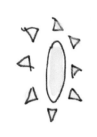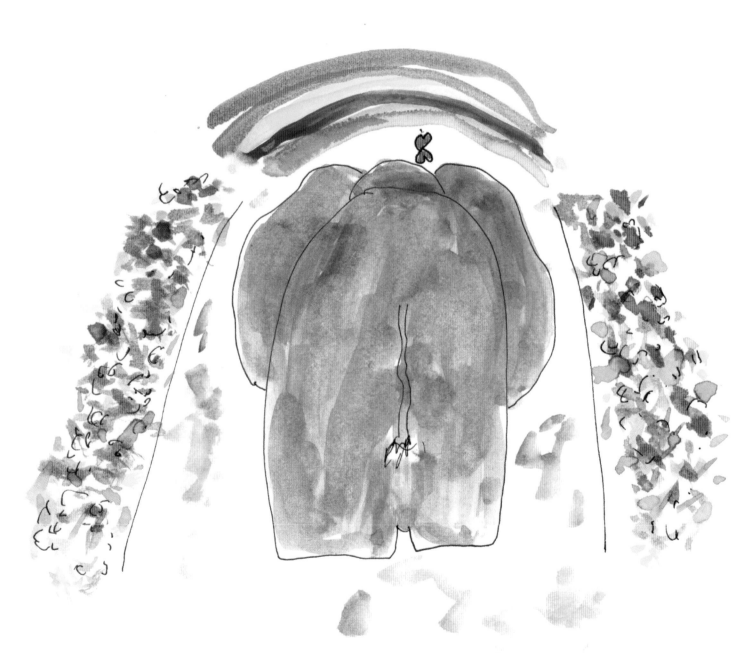

The end.